The Flight of the
SNOW GOOSE

For my mother. 1996.

The Moon and the Stars are for Lauren.

Special thanks to Gina Pollinger, the Wildfowl and Wetlands Trust at Slimbridge,
and film producer Steve Nicholls for ideas and inspiration.

This edition published in Picture Lions in Great Britain by HarperCollins Publishers Ltd 1999.
First published in hardback by HarperCollins Publishers Ltd 1997.
1 3 5 7 9 10 8 6 4 2
ISBN 0 00 664 590-9
Picture Lions is an imprint of the Children's Division, part of HarperCollins Publishers Ltd,
77-85 Fulham Palace Road, Hammersmith, London, W6 8JB

Printed and bound in Singapore by Imago

The Flight of the
SNOW GOOSE

DEBORAH KING

PictureLions

An Imprint of HarperCollinsPublishers

While the city sleeps
in the still of the night,
the white birds of winter
make their flight.

In unwavering lines
they pass by the moon,
whispering their song
from the stars.

A child wakes
to the magical sound.
She counts thousands of birds
southward bound.

Where do they come from?
Where do they go?
These travellers of the night.

They fly from the north
    to escape the snows,
from the edge of the earth
where nobody goes,
from the frozen wastes
where the polar bear prowls
and the lone wolf howls to the moon.

Their lives stretch out
over thousands of miles,
governed by seasons
guided by stars.

Their ancient migrations
are older than nations;
their wings beat a rhythm through time.

They fly high through the clouds
in the cool crisp air.
They cross tundra and forest
in the realm of the bear.

But where are the buffalo?

And where are the Sioux,

who listened on the wind for their song?

The prairies have gone
and machines work the land.
Crops are sown,

grain is grown,

a new landscape is planned.

Then a crack fills the air.
Geese fall to the gun,

twisting and tumbling

one by one.

The survivors move south
to safer ground,
the sound of their voices
drifting down,
waking the children
who want to know...

Where do they come from?
Where do they go?

If they follow the song

of the geese

in full flight

as they pass over cities

and highways

at night,

they will see them come down

in a blizzard of white

falling like snow

on the lakes

at first light.

As they lift off once more
and circle around

in a rush of wings

and a whirlpool of sound,

they fill the skies

with patterns

and lines,

leading up

leading off

to their wintering grounds.

They head south to the sun
for a season of rest,
to Whispering Water,
a vast wilderness.
A valley of peace in New Mexico
in the land of the Pueblo tribes.

But when the north wind calls
from far away,
the geese become restless,
they know not to stay.

By the moon and the stars
they must find their way
and return to their Arctic home.

Their song wakes the land
from its long winter sleep.
The sun breaks the ice
and the ice retreats.

A new year begins,
another cycle complete
in the lives of the migrating geese.

In the melting snow
where the river flows
to the edge of the world
where nobody goes,
the white birds of winter
raise their young
in the land of the midnight sun.

MIGRATION AND THE SNOW GEESE

Migration is one of the most awe inspiring events of the natural world. How can these birds, without compass, without maps, cover such enormous distances? How do they know where they are going?

No one knows the answers for sure, but we have managed to trace their journeys over whole continents. Just as an aircraft follows a flight path, it seems that there are flyways for birds, giant maps which they follow year after year.

The snow goose is a relentless traveller. The birds nest in the far north of Russia and Canada and the goslings hatch out during the Arctic summer. Within a few weeks they have made their first journey with their parents to the tundra wetlands, where there is plenty of food and twenty-four hours of daylight in which to graze. But they have not much time. Winter arrives early in the north and soon the snow geese must travel south or starve.

With the arrival of the first snow, the geese take to the air. Some of the Russian birds fly to the north of Alaska and from there make a non-stop flight all the way along the Pacific coast to California. As many as two million birds will take the central flyway across the Canadian forests and farmlands of America, all the way down the eastern side of the Rockies. Tired and hungry, the birds are easy targets for any hunter. Often they fly at night, stopping only briefly for a rest on lakes or wetlands. They fly in a long, straggling line, or in a V-shape, taking it in turns to be leader. Finally, after a journey of nearly three thousand miles, they arrive at their winter homes in California and the Gulf states and as many as 40,000 birds choose the welcoming reserve of Bosque del Apache which borders the Rio Grande river in New Mexico. Others will continue even further south to Mexico.

But they do not rest for long. Three months later at the first sign of spring, they take off for the northern skies on another long and dangerous journey to the Arctic to raise a new generation of snow geese.

Today, people are trying to help them on their journey. They have created new reserves and replaced some of the old watering holes on the migration routes. They have even begun to plant special fields of corn for the birds. Although a fifth of their number are lost to hunters each year, the flocks of snow geese are increasing and they are able to continue their ancient pattern of migration across America.